W9-CND-015

Cecily G. and the 9 monkeys

Copyright © 2007 by Houghton Mifflin Harcourt Publishing Company
Copyright © 1942 by H. A. Rey. Copyright © renewed 1969 by H. A. Rey
Afterword copyright © 2007 by Louise Borden
Curious George® and related characters, created by Margret and H. A. Rey,
are copyrighted and trademarked by Houghton Mifflin Harcourt Publishing Company.

All rights reserved. For information about permission to reproduce selections from
this book, write to Permissions, Houghton Mifflin Harcourt Publishing Company,
215 Park Avenue South, New York, New York 10003.

www.hmhbooks.com

Library of Congress Cataloging-in-Publication Data

Rey, H. A. (Hans Augusto), 1898–1977.
[Cecily G. and the 9 monkeys]
Curious George : Cecily G. and the 9 monkeys /
written and illustrated by H. A. Rey ; afterword by Louise Borden.
p. cm.
Summary: A lonely giraffe teams up with the nine playful monkeys.
ISBN-13: 978-0-618-80066-7 (hardcover)
ISBN-13: 978-0-618-99794-7 (paperback)
[1. Giraffe—Fiction. 2. Monkeys—Fiction.] I. Title.
II. Title: Cecily G. and the nine monkeys.
PZ7.R33Ce 2007
[E]—dc22   2006038698

Printed in China

WKT 10 9 8 7 6 5 4 3 2 1

PHOTO CREDITS:
Bettman/CORBIS: p. 44 (top)
CORBIS: p. 44 (bottom)
H. A. & Margret Rey Papers, the de Grummond Children's Literature Collection,
University of Southern Mississippi: pp. 35 (top and bottom), 43
Hulton-Deutsch Collection/CORBIS: pp. 37, 42 (bottom)

Cecily G. and the 9 monkeys

by H. A. Rey

Afterword by Louise Borden

Houghton Mifflin Harcourt
Boston • New York

Here are the names of the nine monkeys in this book:

Mother Pamplemoose and **Baby Jinny**

Curious George who was clever, too

James who was good

Johnny who was brave

Arthur who was kind

David who was strong

and **Punch** and **Judy,** the twins

This is Cecily G. Her whole name is Cecily Giraffe, but she is called Cecily G. or just plain Cecily for short.

One day she was very sad because all her family and all her friends had been taken away to a zoo. Cecily G. was all alone. She began to cry because she wanted someone to play with.

Now, in another place,
lived a mother monkey called
Mother Pamplemoose and eight little monkeys. They were
sad, too, because some woodcutters had cut down all the trees
in their forest, and monkeys have to have trees to live in. One
of the little monkeys was called Curious George. He was a
clever monkey. He said, "We must pack up at once and go on
a journey to find a new home."

So they did. They walked and they walked and they walked
until they came to the bank of a deep river. They couldn't get
across and there wasn't any way around. They didn't know
what to do.

Suddenly Jinny, the baby monkey, pointed across to the other bank.

There stood Cecily Giraffe! When she saw the monkeys, she stopped crying. "Do you want to get across?" she said.

"Yes, yes!" they cried.

"Step back then," called Cecily G.

Yoop! With one big jump Cecily's front feet landed on the monkeys' side of the bank. And then she stood still.

Curious George was the first to see that Cecily had made
herself into a bridge. He ran across. Then came Johnny, who
was a brave monkey. Then all the others, one by one.

"Thank you, dear Giraffe," shouted George, "and please
put your head down a little so that we can talk to you without
shouting. That's better! What is your name and why are you
sad?"

"My name is Cecily Giraffe, and I am unhappy because I
haven't anyone to play with. Why are *you* sad?"

"We are sad," said George, "because we haven't anywhere
to live."

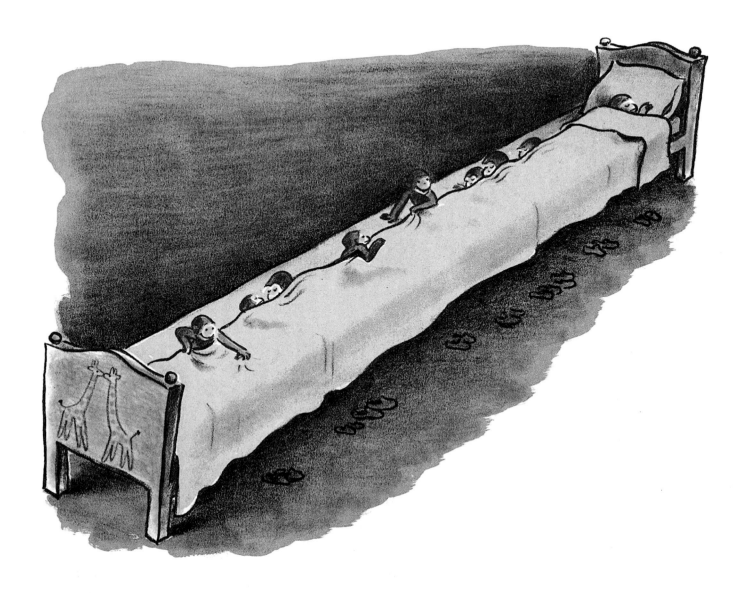

"Then why don't you stay with me for a while?" said Cecily. "My house is empty now."

"We'd love to," cried all the monkeys at once.

"Good!" said Cecily, and she smiled for the first time that day. "Now it is bedtime. I'll show you your room, and tomorrow we'll have some lovely games." So she tucked all the nine monkeys into one giraffe bed, and in a few minutes they were fast asleep.

Next morning, after a good night's sleep and a big break-
fast, Cecily G. said, "Now let's play see-saw! James, you sit on
my back. (James was a very good monkey and usually had first
turn.) George, you climb on my head, and you, Johnny, sit on
my hind feet. That's the way!"

"Now," they cried, "off we go!" Cecily stood up on her
front legs. Up-down, up-down, up-down, went the see-saw.

After a while Cecily stopped and took on another load.
Everyone had a turn; but baby Jinny got so excited that
Mother Pamplemoose was afraid she would fall off. She had
to climb down and give her place to James, who got an
extra ride. Jinny cried a little, but Arthur, who was
very kind, dried her tears and told her that he
had an idea for another game that she
could play better.

So Arthur whispered
something to all the other
monkeys. They rushed into the house
where they had left their belongings and in
a minute they were back with their skis.
"But there isn't any snow for skis," said Cecily G.

"Please," said George, "be so kind as to stretch your neck so I can tie your head to the top of that palm tree over there."

"I'll be glad to," said Cecily, and she did.

Then all the monkeys put on their skis, climbed the tree, and slid down Cecily's back, over and over again. Brave Johnny even did stunts. When he jumped he seemed to be flying.

After a while Cecily's neck got tired, but she was having such a good time that she hardly noticed. "You are a wonderful skier, Johnny," she said.

Johnny was so pleased he tried a specially high jump and—bump—down he fell, flat on his nose.

Mother Pamplemoose ran to pick him up. "I think it is time to play something else," she said. "Let's find a game that Cecily can play too."

"Yes, yes," cried all the monkeys.

Johnny thought very hard because he was such a good
monkey that he wanted Cecily to be sure and have fun, too.
All at once he had a wonderful idea. "We'll make some *stilts*
for Cecily G.," he cried.

Johnny and David, who was a very strong
monkey, cut down two palm trees.
The twins, Punch and Judy,
did the sawing.

James hammered the nails.

George watched and gave advice. When the stilts were done, he proudly carried them to Cecily G. and showed her how to use them.

Cecily Giraffe was terribly excited.

All the monkeys helped and—up—UP—UP—she went—right into the sky—

so high the page isn't big enough to show all of her.

It was very hot the next day and they all thought it would be just the thing to go to the seashore.

After a short walk, they came to the beach and Mother Pamplemoose thought it would be nice to have a swim before lunch. But Johnny had been thinking. He asked Cecily to put down her head so that he could whisper in her ear.

Can you guess what he said? He wanted Cecily to be a—

SAILBOAT! And so Cecily made herself into a sailboat.
Johnny was Captain. He shouted orders and

pulled the ropes. "Not so hard, not so hard!" cried
Cecily. But she was too late—

over they went, into the water.

"Quick, quick, climb on my back," called Cecily Giraffe, when Johnny cried for help.

In a minute they were safe on the beach, but Cecily was so wet and cold, they decided to take off her skin and hang it in the sun to dry.

"It is quite complicated to be a giraffe," said Punch to Judy as they brought Cecily the clothespins.

Cecily Giraffe had hardly gotten her skin back on again when a big black cloud came up and hid the sun.

"Oh—oh—it's going to rain—" cried the monkeys.

Off they rushed, and back they came, one-two, one-two, carrying their umbrellas on their shoulders.

But the rain didn't start at once and James thought it would be fun to use the umbrellas for a new game. He called it "Parachute-jumping."

Each monkey, one at a time, climbed up on Cecily's head, opened his umbrella, and jumped off.

Down they floated. It was such fun they did it hundreds of times.

All went well until, all of a sudden, Curious George tipped his umbrella sideways to see something and—thump—down he fell. When he looked at his broken umbrella, he sat down on the ground to cry. And, just at that moment, the rain started. Poor George! Great splashing drops began to fall around him.

"Quick, quick, climb up my neck, George," said Cecily.

George climbed up and up until he was in the sunshine
again, high above the rain cloud.

All week long Cecily and her new friends had great fun.
When Sunday came, Cecily was so happy she decided to give
a concert to celebrate. The monkeys thought it a splendid
idea. Arthur made up a nice song for them to sing together
and George promised to play on the harp.

At last they were ready and George was just starting
them off when someone cried—

"Fire! Fire! Cecily's house is burning!"

The concert stopped almost before it started, but no one knew what to do to put out the fire.

"If only we had a ladder, we could throw water on the flames," cried Mother Pamplemoose.

"I know what to do," said James. "There's a pump near the house, and a hose, and Cecily can be the ladder."

Punch and Judy worked the pump and—

George climbed up to turn the hose on the fire. James
stood on Cecily's back to guide the hose up to George.

In a minute the fire was out and Cecily's
house was saved.

Cecily looked at the wet little monkeys and said, "Dear
new friends, I don't know how to thank you. . . . Would you
like to stay with me always? It would make me very happy."

"Oh, Cecily G.," cried Mother Pamplemoose, baby Jinny,
curious George, brave Johnny, good little James, kind Arthur,
strong David, and the twins, Punch and Judy, all together,
"we'll stay with you for ever and ever. . . . And now let's finish
our concert."

So they took hold of hands, danced round in a ring,

and sang Arthur's song as loud as they could sing.

Nine lit-tle monks were we home-less and

in di-is – may till Ce-ci – ly Gi-

raff' had us a – long t-o stay

so here in a ri-ing we'll all dance and si-ing

Cec'-ly Cec'ly we will ne-ver go a-way.

The Story Behind the Story of Cecily G.

More than a hundred years ago,
Margarete Waldstein
and Hans Augusto Reyersbach
(known now as H. A. Rey)
were born in Hamburg, Germany.

Growing up,
Margarete and Hans both loved animals.

Hans and his family lived only a few streets
from the famous Hagenbeck Zoo.
There he learned to imitate the roar of a lion,
the bark of a seal,
and the quick chatter of monkeys.
At home,
he spent his free time drawing.

After he grew up,
Hans became a writer and an artist.
So did Margarete,
who attended a famous art school,
the Bauhaus.
There she studied photography.
Soon after this,
Margarete,
who had a mind of her own,
shortened her name to Margret.

Top right: *Margarete Waldstein as a young girl*
Bottom left: *Painting by Hans Reyersbach, 1906*

Hans and Margret were travelers as well,
and during their long lives
the Reys lived in Germany,
then Brazil,
then France,
and then the United States.
Three continents!

Each time they lived in a new city,
Margret and Hans made visits to the local zoo,
and took their camera
and sketchbooks.

In Brazil,
Margret and Hans saw lots of monkeys.
They even had two tiny ones,
called marmosets,
as pets.
There were wide beaches
near the Reys' apartment in Rio de Janeiro . . .
also palm trees,
and the ocean.

On August 16, 1935,

Margret Waldstein and Hans Reyersbach

were married

and became Brazilian citizens.

Hans began to sign his work as H. A. Rey

because his new name was easier for his clients to say,

and to remember.

Months later, in 1936,

the Reys left Rio on a ship,

and headed to Europe for a honeymoon,

where they stayed at the Terrass Hotel in Paris.

Since there were many artists

who also lived in this neighborhood, known as Montmartre,

Margret and H.A. decided to settle in France,

live in their hotel apartment,

and find work.

In elegant Paris,
Hans loved to draw and paint,
and Margret enjoyed words and text.
Sometimes she helped H.A.
to make his watercolor paintings
even better.

Over the next two years,
Hans had a few books published,
but they were for grownups,
not children.

One morning,
Hans sat at his desk
in the Terrass apartment,
smoking his pipe and daydreaming,
as he often liked to do.

Then, to earn some money,
he picked up his pencil
and drew an illustration of a giraffe,
and signed his name,
H. A. Rey.

The picture was full of gentle humor,
because Hans liked people to smile
when they saw his artwork.

H. A. Rey's funny giraffe
was soon printed in a French magazine.

Just days later,
a French editor named Jacques Schiffrin
sat at his desk at Gallimard,
a famous publishing house in Paris,
paging through a magazine.
He stopped reading
and smiled.

What a marvelous giraffe!

Jacques jotted down the artist's name:
H. A. Rey.

Then he called the office
of the Paris magazine
and asked for Monsieur Rey's address
and phone number.
            "Hotel Terrass . . . 12, rue Joseph de . . ."

Jacques Schiffrin was a fine editor,
and he thought this giraffe
could be a character in a book for children.
He was sure that his own son,
little André,
who wasn't old enough to read yet,
would love looking at such a book.

Soon Hans signed a contract with Gallimard
for the Reys' very first book for children.

Top right: *Hotel Terrass*

Margret and H. A. chuckled as they plotted the story
in their room at the Terrass.

Hmm . . .
  The giraffe would be the star,
    and her name would be . . . Rafi.
    Rafi was sad because . . .
    her family had been carried off to . . . to . . .
    a zoo!

Since the Reys loved monkeys,
    and so did children,
Hans drew a mother monkey
and named her
Madame Pamplemoose.

Then he drew her eight children:
Zozo,
Sirocco,
Zig Zag,
Cactus,
Carabaa,
Carabee,
Caraboo,
and Fifi,
who was the youngest monkey.

Hmm . . .

Margret and Hans talked some more,
and slowly built their story,
scene by scene.

On a journey to find a new home,
the monkeys meet Rafi
and have antics with . . .
Hmm . . .
How about skis?
(The Reys had seen skis in Germany.)

And stilts?
(The Reys had seen stilts at the circus.
They both *loved* the circus.)

And parachutes?
(Because *umbrellas* look like parachutes.)
And a fire hose?
(There's always commotion at a fire.)

Since the Reys enjoyed music,
and so do children,
they made up a little song
to include on the last page of their book.

Jacques Schiffrin edited their story and pictures,
and in 1939,
the book was published in France
as *Rafi et les 9 Singes*.

The book had a handsome green cover,
and a few months later,
after World War II began,
it was also published in England
as *Raffy and the Nine Monkeys*.

Margret and Hans had hopes that Raffy
would be published in the United States,
but the war in Europe
made their plan too difficult.

In early June of 1940,
the battles of war were in France,
near Paris.

Thousands,
and then millions,
of French refugees
had to flee
as Hitler's German tanks and troops
swept toward the capital.
Since the Reys had no car
and few trains were running,
Hans hurried to a *velo* shop,
but all the bikes had been sold out.
So he bought spare parts . . .
and assembled two bicycles
all by himself.

Bottom left: *German troops on the march*
Top: *British version of* Raffy and the Nine Monkeys

The next morning at dawn,
Margret and Hans joined the flood of refugees
on the rainy roads south of Paris.
The date was June 12, 1940.

Like the nine monkeys,
the Reys were on their own journey
to find a new home,
but theirs was a much more dangerous one.
Margret and Hans were German-born Jews,
and anyone who was Jewish
was at risk in Hitler's Europe . . .
even those with Brazilian passports.

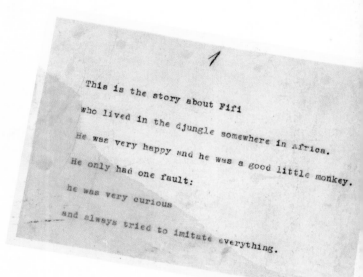

In the baskets strapped to their bicycles
were a few belongings,
a copy of *Raffy and the Nine Monkeys,*
and some unpublished manuscripts,
including a story the Reys were working on
about the monkey Fifi
who had appeared in Raffy's book.

Fifi was the star of this story . . .
he was always getting into mischief,
and he had a friend,
a man with a yellow hat,
who smoked a pipe,
just as Hans did.

Top: *Early manuscript*

By bicycle and train,
and by sleeping in a barn,
in a school,
and on the floor of a restaurant along the way,
Margret and H. A. Rey escaped across the
French border
into Spain
and traveled on to Lisbon, Portugal.

From there they sailed on a ship,
the *Angola,*
to Brazil,
and then took another ship
to New York City.

Finally,
on October 14, 1940,
a cold, sunny day,
the Reys' boat sailed past the Statue of Liberty
into New York Harbor.

A few weeks later,
they met with Grace Hogarth,
an American editor who already knew the Reys,
as she had worked for their publisher in England.
Soon after,
Hans signed a contract for four books,
including the one about the monkey Fifi.

Top right: *German invasion*
Top left: *German troops in France*

Mrs. Hogarth suggested that George
would be a stronger name than Fifi,
so this book was published in 1941
as *Curious George.*

Grace Hogarth also looked through
Raffy and the Nine Monkeys,
which she had read
and admired
when she worked in England.

Now she wanted to publish it in America.

Raffy needed a few changes
to appeal to readers in the United States.
In their apartment in New York City,
Margret and Hans rewrote some of the text
and made up new names for all the characters,
except for one.

Raffy became Cecily G.
(G. for *giraffe*)
and the monkeys became
Baby Jinny,
Curious George,
James,
Johnny,
Arthur,
David,
and Punch and Judy,
who were twins.
Mother Pamplemoose kept her original name.

So . . .

. . . in 1942,
sixty-five years ago,
Cecily G. and the Nine Monkeys
was published in America by Houghton Mifflin,
and has been in print ever since.

How lucky for the Reys,
that one day long ago in Paris,
Hans's drawing of a giraffe
caught the attention of Jacques Schiffrin.

How wonderful that the kind-hearted Rafi,
also known as Raffy,
and now known as Cecily G.,
was with them from the very beginning . . .

along with Mother Pamplemoose's little monkey Fifi,

who later would have his own adventures,

and narrow escapes,

as the beloved Curious George.

And how very remarkable that Hans and Margret

made their wartime journey safely.

They found friendship,

creative work,

and a new home in America.

And like the nine monkeys,

they decided to stay.

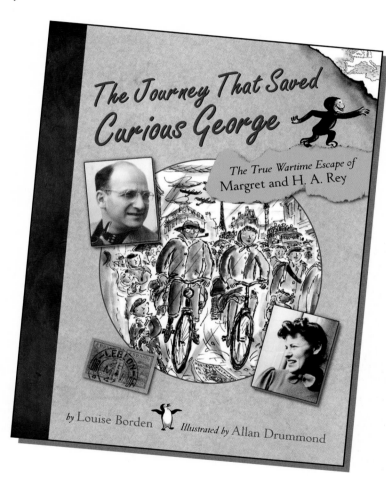

Louise Borden is the author of *The Journey That Saved Curious George: The True Wartime Escape of Margret and H. A. Rey.*